If you walk down a certain road in a certain city in old China, past the pet market with its yellow-and-green ricebirds in their bamboo cages and the goldfish in their porcelain bowls, you will find a little girl named Ruby. Ruby is unlike most girls of her time. Instead of getting married, Ruby is determined to attend university when she grows up, just like the boys in her family.

Inspired by the life of the author's grandmother and paired with evocative watercolor paintings, *Ruby's Wish* is an engaging portrait of a determined young girl and a family who rewards her independent spirit.

❋ Praise for *Ruby's Wish* ❋

"Bridges' lively storytelling turns what could have been just another family story about a feminist on the forefront into a gem." —*San Francisco Chronicle*

★ "This understated tale takes Ruby's predicament seriously while still celebrating her love of learning and her joyful personality." —*Publishers Weekly*, starred review

"Well crafted, admirable, and engaging. . . . A lovely read-aloud with illustrations to linger over."
—*School Library Journal*

"[This] quietly feminist story is complemented by illustrations as graceful as calligraphy strokes."
—*The Horn Book*

"Ruby's determined character will capture the audience's imagination."
—*The Bulletin of the Center for Children's Books*

An Ezra Jack Keats New Illustrator Award winner
An Ezra Jack Keats New Writer Award winner
An Amelia Bloomer List selection
A California Young Reader Medal nominee
A Publishers Weekly Best Children's Book of the Year

Ruby's Wish

To Graeme, for loving my stories—S. Y. B.

To my daughter, Olive, and my dear friend Imogen—S. B.

First Chronicle Books LLC paperback edition, published in 2015.

Originally published in hardcover in 2002 by Chronicle Books LLC.

Text copyright © 2002 by Shirin Yim Bridges.

Illustrations copyright © 2002 by Sophie Blackall.

ISBN 978-1-4521-4569-3

The Library of Congress has cataloged the original edition as follows:

Bridges, Shirin Yim.

Ruby's wish / Shirin Yim Bridges ; [illustrated by] Sophie Blackall.

p. cm.

Summary: In China, at a time when few girls are taught to read or write, Ruby dreams of going to university with her brothers and male cousins.

ISBN-13 978-0-8118-3490-2

ISBN-10 0-8118-3490-5

[1. Sex role-Fiction. 2. Education-Fiction. 3. China-History—19th century-Fiction.]

I. Blackall, Sophie, ill. II. Title.

PZ7.B75234 Ru 2002

[Fic]—dc21

2001007406

Manufactured in China.

FSC MIX
Paper from responsible sources
www.fsc.org FSC™ C008047

Design by Kristen M. Nobles.

Typeset in Hiroshige and Ruling Script

Chinese calligraphy by Jianwei Fong.

The illustrations in this book were rendered in gouache on Arches hot-pressed paper.

10 9 8 7 6 5 4 3

Chronicle Books LLC

680 Second Street

San Francisco, California 94107

Chronicle Books—we see things differently. Become part of our community at www.chroniclekids.com.

Ruby's Wish

by Shirin Yim Bridges   illustrated by Sophie Blackall

chronicle books · san francisco

If you walk down a certain road in a certain city in China, past the pet market with its yellow-and-green ricebirds hopping in their bamboo cages, and the goldfish and the terrapins in their porcelain bowls, you will come to a block of houses, five houses wide and seven houses deep. Many families live here now, and the buildings are brown with age and dirt. But if you look closely, you will see that, once upon a time, this was all one house, the magnificent home of one family.

The house was built by an old man who returned from the Gold Mountain. That was what the Chinese called California, when many men left to join the Gold Rush there and few came back again. But as I said, this man did come back, and he came back very rich. And he did what rich men did in old China: he married many wives. His wives had many sons, and these sons also had many wives. So at one time, the house was filled with the shrieks and laughter of over one hundred children.

Amongst these children was a little girl
that everyone called Ruby, because she
loved the color red. In China, red is the
color of celebration. On New Year's Day,
children receive red envelopes full of
good-luck money. Brides wear red on
their wedding days. But Ruby insisted
on wearing red *every* day. Even when her
mother made her wear somber colors
like all her other cousins, Ruby would
tie up her jet-black hair with red ribbons.

Because he had so many grandchildren, Ruby's grandfather hired a teacher to come to the house. Any grandchild who wanted to learn could join the classes. This was unusual in China in those days, when most girls were never taught to read or write.

Whenever the weather was fine, classes were held in the garden. The windows of Ruby's grandfather's office opened onto that garden. Often, he would rise from his desk to gaze out of his windows at his grandchildren.

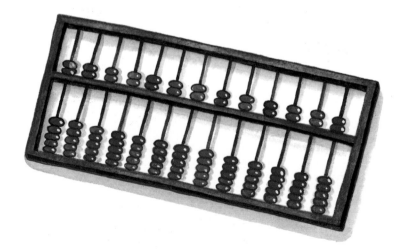

One day, Ruby's grandfather looked down from his window to see the high white wall of the garden plastered with calligraphy. His grandchildren had been practicing their handwriting. Ruby's grandfather laughed to see that many had smudged ink on their hands and faces!

人有朋友

人有朋友

人有朋友

Then he noticed a sheet that was more beautiful than the rest. Which of his grandchildren had produced such wonderful calligraphy? Down in the garden, the teacher was praising Ruby. Her ears were turning as bright red as her jacket.

But if Ruby was doing as well as her boy cousins in her studies, she had to work much harder. When the boys had finished their studies for the day, they were free to play. But the girls had to learn about cooking and keeping house. In fact, as far as their mothers were concerned, these were the *only* things girls had to learn.

One by one, the girls stopped going to the classes. All except Ruby. She would catch up on her embroidery at night. Many nights, her candle flickered long after everyone else had gone to bed.

最
後
不
幸
生
不
幸
生
不
幸
生
不
幸
生

One day, the children were asked
to write a poem. Ruby wrote:

*Alas, bad luck to be born a girl; worse luck to be
born into this house where only boys are cared for.*

Ruby's teacher was very impressed by the poem. He
showed it to Ruby's grandfather. Ruby's grandfather
was also impressed, but he was worried about what
the poem said. He summoned Ruby to his office.

Ruby found her grandfather sitting in his chair, her poem spread open on his desk.

"Did you write this poem?" asked Ruby's grandfather.

"Yes I did, Grandfather," answered Ruby.

"Do you really think that in this house we only care for boys?"

"Oh no, Grandfather," said Ruby, very sorry that she had upset him. "You take good care of all of us, and for that we are all grateful."

"Little Ruby," her grandfather said gently, "I really would like to know why you wrote this poem. How are the boys better looked after?"

"Well," said Ruby, trying to think of a small, unimportant thing, "when it is the Moon Festival and we are each given half a moon cake, the boys always get the half with the yellow moon yolk."

"Hmmm," said her grandfather, as if he was still waiting. "Is that so?"

"Yes," continued Ruby, "and when it is the Lantern Festival, the girls are given simple paper lanterns but the boys have red lanterns in the shapes of goldfish, cockerels and dragons."

Ruby's grandfather chuckled. He'd never thought about it before. He could imagine how much Ruby would have liked a red lantern.

"But most importantly," said Ruby, staring hard at her red shoes, "the boys will get to go to university, but the girls will be married."

"Don't you want to be married?" asked her grandfather. "You know, you are very lucky. A daughter of this house can marry any man."

"I know, Grandfather," said Ruby, "but I'd much rather go to university."

Ruby's grandfather touched her hair. "Thank you for talking to me, Ruby," he said. "Go on with your lessons. Make the most of them while you can."

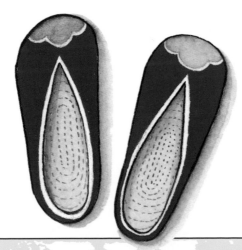

So Ruby went on with her lessons. Some of the boys grew up and went away to university. Some stayed in the house and started families of their own. But when they grew up, all the girls were married and sent away to live in their husbands' homes. Ruby knew it would soon be her turn. In the ponds, Ruby could see the orange-and-white carp gulping for breath under a thin layer of ice. It would soon be Chinese New Year. Ruby felt sure it would be her last one at home.

On New Year's Day, Ruby put on red velvet shoes and tied red ribbons in her hair. Then she went to wish everyone a happy new year. She started with her married cousins, then worked her way up through her parents, aunts and uncles. Each one gave her a red packet full of lucky money. Finally, she bowed before her grandfather. "Good luck and prosperity, Grandfather," she said.

"Good luck, little Ruby," replied her grandfather, and he handed her a very fat red packet.

Ruby could feel the eyes of all her family on her as she opened the lucky red envelope. Can you guess what was in it? It wasn't money, it was something much better than that.

It was a letter from a university, saying that they would be proud to accept Ruby as one of their very first female students.

So that's how Ruby got her wish. It's a true story. And how do I know this? Well, Ruby is my grandmother, and every day she still wears a little red.

Shirin Yim Bridges is an award-winning author and publisher of many books for young readers. In her spare time, she speaks about writing and publishing at such venues as the Asian Festival of Children's Content, the San Francisco Writing Salon, the Australian Society of Children's Book Writers and Illustrators, and Stanford University. She lives in Foster City, California.

Sophie Blackall has illustrated more than thirty books for children, including *Big Red Lollipop*, *Pecan Pie Baby*, and the best-selling Ivy and Bean series. Her own daughter, who was a little girl when this book first came out, is about to go away to university. Just like Ruby, her favorite color is red.